RONNIE & THE CHIEF'S SON

BY ELIZABETH COATSWORTH

Ronnie and the Chief's Son
Indian Encounters

Alice All-By-Herself
The Captain's Daughter
The Cat and the Captain
The Cat Who Went to Heaven
Dancing Tom
Dollar for Luck
The Golden Horseshoe
The House of the Swan
The Little Haymakers
The Littlest House
The Peddler's Cart
Sword of the Wilderness
Thief Island
Trudy and the Tree House
Twelve Months Make a Year

Poems
Summer Green

Away Goes Sally
The Fair American
Five Bushel Farm

First Adventure
The Wishing Pear
Boston Bells
Aunt Flora
Old Whirlwind
The Sod House
Cherry Ann and the Dragon Horse

Ronnie
and the Chief's Son

by Elizabeth Jane Coatsworth

illustrated by Stefan Martin

THE MACMILLAN COMPANY · NEW YORK
MACMILLAN NEW YORK · LONDON · 1962

Library of Congress catalog card number: 62–10637

First Printing

The Macmillan Company, New York
Macmillan New York, London
Brett-Macmillan Ltd., Galt, Ontario
Printed in the United States of America

To Harold, Mark and Henry,
with their grandmother's love.

The boy's name was Ronnie and he was an only child. He was used to being much by himself. Animals meant as much to him as people: his mother's cat, the dogs that his father took with him on lion hunts, the horses they rode were all loved friends. Most of the strangers he saw were also animals, so that he watched less for people than for a glimpse of the elephants, the zebras or the greater and lesser antelopes as they drifted across his father's lands in search of water or new grass in their season. They

followed their own roads, older than the oldest story told by the oldest African in the oldest man-made clearing. They came and passed like migrations of birds. All his life, Ronnie had marked the seasons by these great travelers.

The coming of the bullocks with their dark herders was different. Some years, when the rains had been heavy, they did not come at all. But this year they came on their journey home just before the rains began. Early one morning Ronnie was on his way to see a day-old colt, when his ear caught the sound of far-off lowing and the ringing of copper bells, and, shading his eyes, he could make out the long unfurling pennant of dust that marked the coming of the cattle.

"The bullocks are coming!" he shouted to his father and then ran back to the house to let his mother know. In a few minutes they were all three in the saddle and riding to meet the herd. First came the chief's favorite ox, his horns, with their vast five-foot spread, painted orange and hung with bells and red leather tassels. There were more bells and tassels at his throat. On either side, but a little behind him, walked the bullocks belonging to the two young sons of the chief and after them came the rest of the cattle.

I

They were of all colors, and the shapes of their horns were never alike, though all were enormous. Some rose up into the air, curved like lyres. Some spread sideways into a scimitar sweep like the horns of wild buffalo, and some grew forward in upturned spikes.

Here and there a bullock had been tattooed or painted, and these creatures, too, wore bells and tassels in their degree, for each was a man's favorite animal, the one given to him in his youth as the beginning of his herd. These were not cattle to be fattened for food, but the pride of the herders, whose whole lives from boyhood to old age were given over to their care and safekeeping. A man was often known by his most famous bullock, and might be called "Master of the Spotted Ox," or "Lord of Him Who is Gray as Mist."

The chief and Ronnie's father exchanged greetings. Permission to graze the herd for a few days on his father's lands was asked and granted. The herders then spread out their cattle to feed and made their camp not far behind Ronnie's house, at the edge of the narrow strip of jungle along the river.

Ronnie watched camp being made. The herders leaned their spears against a tree, spread their cloaks on the ground for beds, and, lighting a little fire, were at once at home. There were no women in the party. The women stayed in their villages and worked in their little fields and gardens and tended the goats and cows while the men wandered, sometimes a hundred miles or more, grazing their beloved bullocks.

But if there were no women, there were several boys and two of these were the chief's sons. One was about Ronnie's age and the other was a little older. Ronnie looked at them with interest, but although he and the younger boy exchanged smiles, he could not catch the older one's eye, and before he could talk with them, his father and the chief finished speaking and Ronnie had to ride away.

That night Ronnie dreamed of cattle, flowing like a river over the plain to the sound of their lowing and the little copper bells. Suddenly the lowing of the bullocks changed to a loud bellowing and they seemed to be charging down upon him, their great horns brandished like swords. In his dream Ronnie tried to run, but the earth seemed to clutch at his feet, so that he scarcely could move, and he saw the bellowing, frothing herd like a wave about to break over his head. Before it reached him, Ronnie woke, but the dream remained so real and terrifying that instead of riding out that morning to watch the grazing bullocks as he would ordinarily have done, he decided to go fishing and to think of other things.

His father was already away superintending the clearing of new land some miles from the house, but his mother readily gave Ronnie permission to take his lunch to the river so that he might stay as long as he liked. Walking through the strip of jungle that bordered the riverbank, he saw that some of his father's men were cutting down trees for a new horse corral that his father meant to have built. Usually Ronnie would have stopped to watch them, but on this day, for some reason, he wanted to be alone. If being alone was really what he wanted, he had chosen the wrong place and time, for he had scarcely baited his hook when there was a movement near him, and the younger of the chief's sons appeared, smiling shyly. Ronnie, instead of being annoyed, was very pleased. In five minutes the boys were talking as if they had known one another half their lives and Ronnie insisted that the other boy should take the rod and fish while he watched. Once Ronnie asked him where his brother was. His new friend didn't look up from the hook he was baiting. "How should I know?" he answered. "He is the son of the head wife. He scarcely speaks to me."

They fished all morning, turn and turn about, and the chief's son caught one large river catfish with which he was very pleased. When they grew hungry they shared Ronnie's food, and soon, being still hungry, wandered off, side by side, to get something more to eat at the house.

As they came into the clearing in the jungle where the cutting was being done, they caught a glimpse of the chief's older son watching the men at work. Suddenly the men yelled to him to get out of the way, as a tree was about to fall. The boy looked at them haughtily. He was not accustomed to be yelled at, nor to run when ordered. He was a chief's son.

But the tree had no respect for anyone. It came down with a tearing scream, its branches flailing out as it fell. The end of a large limb caught the boy and he was dead when the others reached him.

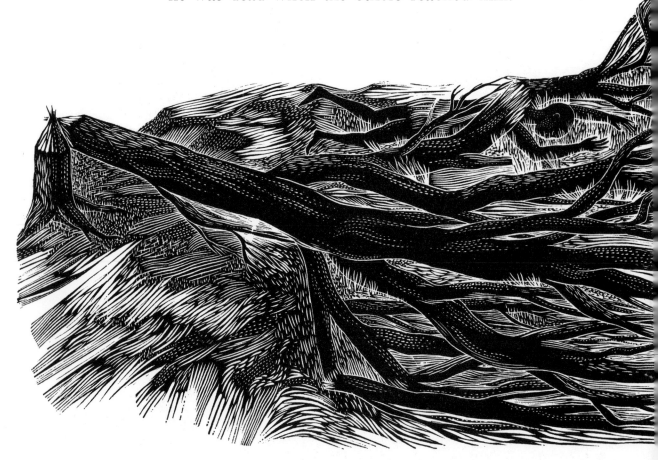

After that things happened fast. Ronnie later could never remember exactly the order of events. He noticed the catfish lying ugly and neglected on the earth; he heard the frightened talk of the woodcutters, and then his friend's voice as he began the mourning chant for his older brother.

"I must let the chief know," Ronnie thought. No one saw him start off at a steady trot toward where the herd was grazing. He could never have told whether it was a long time or a short time before he found the chief and saw the courteous welcome wiped from his face by sorrow and anger.

"Your father has taken my son. I shall take his," the man said, and gave a few orders before he strode off with two or three of his followers toward the jungle glade where his dead son and his living son waited for him. Ronnie started to follow, but at once dark hands seized him and a cloth was bound across his mouth. Next he found himself being half-led, half-carried into the center of the grazing herd. All about him were the bullocks, so large that their backbones came higher than the top of his head. He could see nothing but their many-colored hides, their patient heads and heavy horns. Gently they made way for

Ronnie and the men who held him, and like water they closed in again when they had passed. He had been badly frightened when the herdsmen caught hold of him, but now he felt his fear dying away, surrounded as he was on every side by the massive calm of the cattle. All about him he heard their breathing. Now and then one stretched out its head, its thin dewlap rippling, and lowed peacefully, and as they fed, the little bells tinkled and tankled in a hundred tones. These animals, which had always been treated as precious possessions, breathed out peace and power, and, frightened as Ronnie was, he was quieted by this great pool of content in which he was submerged.

By now only one herder had remained with him, a thin, middle-aged man who kept his knife in his hand, although when he spoke to Ronnie there was nothing fierce in his face or voice.

"You will stay here all day while the bullocks graze, all night while they sleep, but no harm will come to you. When your father returns, he will search for you, but what the cattle hide, they hide well. There are no footprints where the herd has passed. Their bodies are a wall to the keenest gaze. And sound— you will make none," and the man moved the hand with the dagger just a little.

Late that afternoon, having been summoned home to a frantic house, Ronnie's father visited the herd as it grazed slowly toward its village.

"Why should I know?" asked the chief to his questions. "My son is dead. You see his body swinging there in his cloak between the horns of his bullock. But your son? What should I have to do with him? You say he was by the river. A crocodile may have taken him. Or a leopard. Ask them and not me."

Ronnie's father tried to talk to the other herdsmen. He offered them money with which to buy more bullocks, he threatened and stormed, but they only looked stupid and had the same answer. He shouted Ronnie's name but the knife was at Ronnie's back and the boy dared not answer. Then Ronnie's father pushed his way here and there among the cattle, but it was like parting quicksilver which comes together again as soon as separated. Once indeed he came near Ronnie and a terrible game of hide and seek took place, for as he came closer, Ronnie was forced to slip away unseen between ox and ox, the tip of the knife pricking his back.

And so at last, brokenhearted and against his will, Ronnie's father grew convinced that his son was not with the herders, but had indeed been drowned while fishing, or taken by a crocodile, lord of the river, or

by a leopard, lord of the jungles, or even by the wandering lion, recently heard roaring at nightfall not far from the native encampment.

He did not, however, easily give up the hope that Ronnie might be with the herd. Five times he overtook the cattle. Five times he and his men searched.

The last time he came, he rode up to the encampment at a gallop, late in the night, thinking perhaps to discover his son sleeping with the others by the fire. But he found no son, only the chief and his companions, wrapped each in a hide, asleep or just waking in the last glow of the embers. There were two or three boys among them. He looked anxiously into each face. None was Ronnie's. Then he rode away on the long, long ride home and after that he gave up hope and did not return again.

That night Ronnie did not even know that his father had come. As always, he was made to sleep among the sleeping bullocks, those great creatures which permitted him to warm himself, lying at their sides, or half reclining in the arc of one of their strong throats. While it was still dark, before dawn, the herd always rose and once again began to feed, and Ronnie, half asleep, with his guard, was forced to rise with them, wandering slowly, often with a sleepy arm flung about one of the animals' necks.

If Ronnie endured his captivity without terror or
loneliness, it was because of the bullocks. They
showed him no particular affection, he was just a
boy to them like the herdboys, but they had an utter
trust in people, and their ways were slow and kind
as the ways of orchard trees might be, if they walked
about on earth.

Ronnie kept no track of time but it was perhaps
two weeks before they reached the chief's village.
The women and children and dogs came a long way
across the plains to meet them, and there was much
wailing and outcry when they saw the burden hung
between the horns of the bullock that had belonged to
the chief's eldest son.

15

The village itself was made up of separate enclosures of whitened mud with beehive huts and granaries within. They were owned by the women, each mother of the family being ruler of her own little kingdom within the walls. The bullocks were the pride and occupation of the men. The women owned the houses, the melon and casava patches, the goats and cows. For months on end they lived without men except for a few oldsters, too aged or lame to undertake the wonderful yearly journey of the herd.

Ronnie was given a little hut of his own at the edge of the village where he lived with one or another of his guards. It was the guest house used when strangers stayed overnight with the chief. The round white walls on the outside of the hut were painted with bullocks and lions and a rabbit larger than any of the other animals. Inside, mats were spread at night on the hard clean floor of trampled earth, and outside his door, melon vines gave a touch of green. Not far away, under a great tree, there was a spring and a small stream where the village got its water. Around it stood carved images and the women had tied colored rags in the great branches of the tree. His guard told him that the spring belonged to a good spirit and that it never ran dry, and here Ronnie went every day with a big calabash to fill with water. Often he met other people from the village at the spring but they never spoke to him. He had been there for several days before having his first glimpse of the chief's younger son, with whom he had fished and shared bread on the unlucky day of the accident. They had seemed to become friends immediately but now the other boy, stopping to drink at the spring, pretended not to see Ronnie, who was waiting his turn, with a guard loitering near. But as the chief's son bent over the water he spoke, so low that it was not until afterwards that Ronnie, hearing the echo of the words in his memory, knew what he had said:

"You are in great danger. Beware the new moon. I will help you if I can."

In a moment the boy was gone and Ronnie knelt to fill his gourd, his thoughts in a turmoil. So he was in danger. The idea, of course, was not new to him. At any time he had expected to be killed in revenge for the young chief's death, but as day followed day he had begun to wonder if perhaps the chief's anger might not have cooled. He had heard that sometimes a person was adopted into a tribe in the place of someone who had recently died, and he had wondered if that was to be his life.

But his friend had said "Danger." His friend! Here, where no one used him cruelly, no one was kind, either. Now for the first time someone had spoken to him as if he wished him well. "I will help you if I can." Ronnie felt his heart grow warm with gratitude. The village around him seemed less like some dream, where he wandered, unseen and unheard by the other people in the dream.

"New moon!" Ronnie had not noticed the moon very much, but as he thought back, he remembered lying one night against the flank of a big red bullock and looking up into the sky. The crescent moon hung there among the African stars, no longer new, but as yet not much thickened. The chief's son had died, then, at the time of a new moon. And at the next new moon his own spirit would be offered to the spirit of the dead boy to appease its anger.

That night Ronnie lay awake many hours waiting to see the moon through the doorway of his hut. When at last it appeared, it had the sad look of a waning moon already well past the half. Every night, anxiously waking up in the dark, he watched it grow smaller, and thinner and thinner. Then one night it was gone. The stars had the darkness to themselves. When it should reappear, thin as the thinnest knife blade, Ronnie knew that he was to die.

It was very hard to go on quietly living from day to day now, knowing that the days would be so few. And yet the hours seemed endless. Ronnie thought a great deal about home and about his father and mother, the people on the farm, and the animals that were part of the household almost as much as the people were. To fill the time, he began to wander more about the village with one guard or another at his

heels. He would stop to watch two little goats playing together, or an old woman digging in her garden, or a rooster crowing from the stump of a tree. No one ever spoke to him. It was as if he were already an unseen spirit wandering among them, and, if he stopped, no one tried to drive him away. One day he paused to watch a group of boys about his own age playing some game. The chief's son was among them, but he, too, did not seem to see Ronnie as he stood there staring at them sadly.

Yet, just as Ronnie turned to go, the other boy ran up near him and stood panting, resting his hand against a tree trunk as if he needed to catch his breath after the violence of the play. His head was turned away from Ronnie yet suddenly Ronnie realized that he was speaking in quick words between his pantings:

"The rains . . . have come . . . in the north. . . . The great . . . antelopes . . . are moving."

Then, having apparently recovered his breath, still without a glance at Ronnie, the chief's son ran back into the game and, after watching a little longer, Ronnie drifted on in his aimless wandering about the village.

Now he had something new to think about. What could the great antelopes mean to him? The rains had been expected. That was why the herders had brought their bullocks back to their village where there would soon be plenty of grazing. And with the rains the antelopes, great and small, would be moving. How well Ronnie knew their age-old track which crossed the outer edge of his father's land! How often he had ridden out to watch their passing, group after group floating by like the shadows of clouds, stopping now and then to graze or to rest at noonday in the coolness of bush or rock, but always moving onward in the same direction. Yet what could they mean to him now?

When Ronnie woke at night, fearfully looking for the new moon, he usually heard the roar of lions about the village. Because of them, the number of the night herders had been increased. Small fires glared in the darkness all night long in a broken ring about the cattle, and men watched by them, spears in hand. Two or three young animals had indeed been taken, and a lioness had been killed. Sometimes Ronnie had thought that he would try to escape, to slip away in the darkness when for a moment his guard's attention was turned to something else. In his heart he had known how quickly and surely the village hunters would track him down, and now the night-prowling lions made him put away the dream altogether.

Late one afternoon, looking up by long habit, Ronnie saw the new moon. The sight came almost as a relief. The waiting was over. Whatever was going to happen would happen now.

The boy was not the only one to see that thread of light in the clear sky. Almost immediately a group of village women came and, laughing and talking, rubbed his body with oil and wreathed his head and throat with flowers. They were all friendliness now. Each treated him as though he were her favorite child, bringing him fruit and casava cakes, and finally a curious sweet drink in a coconut shell. He was thirsty and drank it to the last drop and almost immediately his fear left him. He felt excited and gay. Something was going to happen to him? What did he care for that? The drums in the village dancing place were beginning to beat, big drums and little drums throbbing together. Ronnie's heart throbbed with them, faster and faster.

Now the people were coming out of their houses, in their best clothes with flowers in their hair. They were all laughing and talking and calling to Ronnie.

"Come along, White Chief's son! Come along, you with the eyes like the sky and the straight back! Hurry up! The dancing is beginning!"

For days and days no one had spoken to Ronnie except his guards and they had said only the few things necessary: his guards and the chief's son, speaking those few broken sentences. Now he was surrounded by friendliness. In his present mood it filled him with joy. Night had fallen, and the flames of the torches, stuck into the earth around the square, seemed to leap and dance to the rhythm of the drums, and everyone else was dancing, too, the chief and his son, the warriors, the women and the children. "Dance! dance!" they cried to Ronnie, catching him by the hands and drawing him into their circle. After all the days of being alone, he was suddenly one of them, laughing and dancing with them, while the garland about his neck swayed to and fro, and his hair kept falling into his blue eyes and his ears were filled with the sound of the drums and of his own laughter.

From time to time he rested and then they brought him more of the sweet drink, which he drank eagerly.

Between the throbbings of the drums he could sometimes hear the gruff roar of a lion, and then again
hands would reach for his hands and again he would
dance and laugh.

Long, long ago the new moon had sunk below
the trees and now the torches were burning low and

the dancers began to edge more and more toward one end of the square where grew a very tall tree with many roots twisting like gray snakes along the ground. Among the roots stood a stone, flat on top, with several carved fetishes about it. Here the torches shone thickest. A circle of old men and women sat among the shadows clapping their hands in time to the dancing, which grew faster and faster as the drums led it, until music and dancing and clapping came in one great wave towering upward, up and up until it must break.

At that moment the foot of a passing dancer tripped Ronnie and he fell sprawling on the ground.

Then, indeed, the wave broke in confusion. The drums faltered, the clapping died away, the dancers stopped in a daze, wiping the sweat from their eyes. Splitting the crowd, the chief appeared, shaken by fury, demanding what had happened. While Ronnie picked himself up, the chief's son admitted his clumsiness and begged his father's forgiveness. Silently the chief turned away and went to his hut, and the throng thinned like water falling on hot sand. The chief was gone, his son was gone, the friendly men, the laughing women, the children who had crowded to be near Ronnie were gone, without a greeting or a word of farewell.

Ronnie was left once more, ghostly and deserted, with only his guard beside him, the torches burned almost out, and the first pallor of false dawn appearing in the east.

With the shock of his fall, the gaiety and courage had been knocked out of Ronnie. Now he was only himself again, tired, bewildered and forlorn. The guard must have been even more tired. As they walked back to Ronnie's hut, the man kept stumbling and his head rolled from side to side.

Ronnie had scarcely lifted the curtain across his door, before the guard lowered himself to the ground and with his head against the painted wall, fell fast asleep. That sudden sleep was one more strange thing in a night which was all strange. The entire village had been drinking from the coconut shells between their bouts of dancing, but only the guard seemed to be affected in this way.

Why was he, Ronnie, still alive? He had not expected to be, but here he was. Here he was, and very, very tired. He would sleep now and in the morning try to understand what had happened.

But the answer to his question did not wait until morning. It came almost at once in a thin shadow slipping along in the darkness of the walls, and appearing at Ronnie's side before he had time to know what had surprised him.

"Quick! quick! the great antelopes have already come to drink at the spring! Cover yourself with this. They will follow this odor anywhere. With the antelopes you will be safe and they will take you home."

As he spoke, the chief's son was rubbing some strange-smelling ointment over Ronnie's hands and arms, his face and his long legs, and after the first bewilderment, Ronnie was helping him, dipping his hands into a calabash filled with a salve whose smell was unlike any smell Ronnie had ever known.

"The guard?" he asked as they worked.

"He will wake tomorrow with a sore head. I put something in his drink which gives one the little death."

"Why did you trip me, Chief's Son?"

"To save you, of course. The sacrifice must come to the stone willingly as you were coming. But when you fell, the omens became bad. My father means now to wait until the next new moon."

There was no time for further talk. The top of the gourd was fitted back into place, leaving half the ointment unused, and so handed to Ronnie.

"Save it for as long as you can," his friend whispered. "You will need it later."

A lion roared, not far from the village.

"The lions?" Ronnie asked in a low voice.

"You are safe with the big antelopes," said the other boy. "Never leave the antelopes, my brother."

"My life is your gift, my brother," said Ronnie.

Presently they were at the spring, but they were not alone. Twenty antelopes were drinking there, noble figures with long spiral horns showing faintly in the coming dawn. When they smelled the ointment they crowded about Ronnie without fear, stretching out their narrow muzzles to sniff at him, and as they smelled this scent which so pleased them, more and more of the creatures appeared silently along the antelope trail, drawn to Ronnie as to a magnet.

The chief's son pressed a leather bag filled with dried meat and casava bread into Ronnie's hand. It was fastened with long thongs so that he might tie it with the ointment gourd over his shoulder.

"Go now!" the chief's son said. "The beasts will follow. This morning the village will sleep late. I have made offerings for you. All will be well." And before Ronnie could thank him again, he was gone, disappearing between antelope and antelope into the shadows.

"Go now!" he had said and Ronnie knew that it was indeed time to be gone. He started off, walking not too fast to keep up the pace for many miles, and the antelopes went with him, so close that he put his hands on the backs of two of them to help himself along the way. By now there must have been more than a hundred of the beautiful creatures. The village stood among trees but soon they came to the plain and there in the brightening day, stood a lion and two lionesses barring their way.

But the great antelopes never hesitated. At the same

pace they went on, without veering, the leaders snort-ing and pawing a little as they advanced. The lions knew those sharp horns, those cutting hoofs and it was they who gave ground, pretending to have no interest in the passers-by.

"So," thought Ronnie, "these are good friends to be with! If only the chief's son were here, too!"

This was for Ronnie the beginning of a strange and legendary journey. As he had traveled to the village against his will in the midst of the gentle bullocks, so now freely he traveled homeward with the antelopes. Their beauty was not in painted horns and tinkling bells and majestic pace but in their wildness, their quick grace, their awareness of every change of wind and every possible danger. The bullocks trusted to their herders, but the antelopes trusted to their keen scent, their eyesight, and their listening ears to warn them, and to their speed or courage in fight to bring them through in times of danger. Their great eyes saw very well in the night and it was then that they did most of their traveling along their ancestral road.

By day they browsed, always moving slowly toward their goal, or rested in the shadow of rocks or thorn bushes, and then Ronnie was glad to rest, too, and to sleep a little. As the ointment began to wear away, he found that the antelopes became shy of him, snorting and drawing back from his touch. When this happened, he used a little more of the salve, watching it anxiously as it grew less and less in the gourd. What would happen to him if the antelopes should turn against him? Even if they did him no harm, how could he travel without them through the wilds, unarmed, a helpless dinner for any lion or leopard or jackal that might pass?

But still they went on day after day, Ronnie upheld and guided and protected by the wild herd, so long as he held the magic that enchanted them. They had gone about two thirds of the way to his father's farm when the moment of real danger came for Ronnie.

At this place the plain along which they had been traveling narrowed to a valley about half a mile wide that lay between cliff-sided hills. Through this pass the antelope trail ran and as Ronnie's herd came to its entrance, the animals slowed down to browse and rest during the heat of the day.

Ronnie was napping in the shadow of a tall rock when he happened to notice an antelope near him standing in the attitude of alarm, head thrown back, snuffing the air with eyes staring ahead into the valley. There, with sudden terror, Ronnie saw a line of men stretched from one cliff to the other. They stood perhaps fifty feet apart, and each was armed with a long spear. At first Ronnie hoped that they might be hunters from some other tribe come to intercept the game, but then he saw that they were the

familiar bullock herders and that he was the prey they were after. With their long spears they were prodding the thorn bushes where a fugitive might lie hidden and slowly they were advancing down the pass toward the herd.

By now all the antelopes had taken alarm and, since the enemy was man, they were about to turn and run. Ronnie would be left behind to be routed out of his hiding place by the spears, or, if he should run, to be tracked down by these thin hunters.

There was only one chance. Opening the ointment gourd, Ronnie, still keeping out of sight behind his thorn bush, smeared the last of the precious stuff over his skin.

To the antelopes the scent, as always, was intoxicating. Forgetting their uneasiness, they crowded about the boy and in a press of animal bodies he leaped to his feet and ran straight toward the men and the narrow pass, surrounded, protected, and hidden by the herd.

The astonished men in the center of the line broke and ran for their lives. On the outskirts several threw their spears and later Ronnie pulled one of these from the haunch of a yearling, but in a maddened rush the human blockade was broken, and the

herd went on down the pass and into the plain be-
yond, scarcely slackening its speed. Though Ronnie
was a good runner he could never have kept up, if
he had not thrown an arm about the necks of two of
the antelopes and so been carried with them, scarcely
touching foot to the ground.

Having begun to run, having outfaced that terrible creature, man, the herd stampeded. They ran for miles, carrying Ronnie in their midst, before they slowed down and suddenly began to graze as if nothing had happened. The men made no attempt to follow. They probably never guessed that Ronnie was with the antelopes. They had been stationed at the pass to catch him as he tried to come through, and all they expected to see was the white boy who had lived in their village traveling alone as a fugitive, if some wild animal had not already made a meal of him. They may have stayed there for some days longer until they felt sure that he was not coming, and then they must have gone back to the chief to tell him that the boy was surely dead, killed either by a beast or a night spirit.

As for Ronnie, that was the final danger through which he passed. The scent of the ointment lasted for several days and, when it wore off, the odor of the gourd itself held the herd another day. By the time he came to his father's land, he was still traveling with the antelopes, but they were veering away. He could no longer touch them, yet they were now so used to his presence that as yet they did not attack him nor fear his presence.

When at last he recognized the dear and familiar landmarks, he worked his way to the outskirts of the herd and stood watching as it passed. Several of the beasts turned their heads as they went by, perhaps in dim alarm, perhaps remembering the pleasure he had brought them.

In return for the magic of the chief's son, they had brought Ronnie safely home. He had gone with the bullocks and come back with the antelopes. He had lived among enemies and found a friend. It had been a dangerous but beautiful wayfaring.

Now he was rejoiced to be home once more. As yet, he alone knew that he was home, but everyone would know it soon.

Elizabeth Coatsworth

Elizabeth Coatsworth was born in Buffalo, New York, but before she was six years old she had traveled cross-country to California and half around the world to Egypt and the Nile.

Miss Coatsworth studied two years at the Buffalo Seminary and then attended Vassar and Columbia, where she took an M.A. degree. The next year she spent in the Orient, and later enjoyed long winters in Europe, North Africa, Mexico and Guatemala. *The Cat Who Went to Heaven,* winner of the Newbery Medal in 1931 grew out of her memories of Japan, as the "Sally Books" reflect her love for New England, where she and her husband, Henry Beston, brought up their children and still live for most of the year.

The story of Ronnie, however, is not based on a known locality, but lies in an Africa of the imagination, in which all things are possible, and friendship may come as suddenly and surely as a bird to a branch.

Up to this time, Miss Coatsworth has written over fifty books for boys and girls, as well as half a dozen novels, and an equal number of books of poetry, which remains to this day her favorite form of writing.